KU-131-815

★ Pirate Patch ★

and the

Message in a Bottle

In which the invincible Pirate Patch and Granny Peg fall into a terrible trap and the ingenius Portside digs them out of it.

ABERDEENSHIRE LIBRARY AND
INFORMATION SERVICES

2630743	
HJ	700555
JS	£8.99
	JF

Reading Consultant: Prue Goodwin, Lecturer in Literacy and
Children's Books at the University of Reading

ORCHARD BOOKS
338 Euston Road, London NW1 3BH
Orchard Books Australia
Hachette Children's Books
Level 17/207 Kent Street, Sydney NSW 2000

First published in Great Britain in 2008
First paperback publication 2009

Text © Rose Impey 2008
Illustrations © Nathan Reed 2008

The rights of Rose Impey to be identified as the author and
Nathan Reed to be identified as the illustrator of this Work
have been asserted by them in accordance with the
Copyright, Designs and Patents Act, 1988.

A CIP catalogue record for this book is available from the British Library

ISBN 978 1 84362 977 1 (hardback)
ISBN 978 1 84362 985 6 (paperback)

1 3 5 7 9 10 8 6 4 2
Printed in China

Orchard Books is a division of Hachette Children's Books,
an Hachette Livre UK company.
www.hachettelivre.co.uk

Pirate Patch

and the

Message in a Bottle

Rose Impey   Nathan Reed

ORCHARD BOOKS

"Staggering Starfish!" Patch grumbled. "It isn't fair."

Mum and Dad told Patch he was *too young* to go to sea . . .

And Granny Peg was *too old*!
"This is no life for bold pirates
like us," said Peg.
Patch agreed. He kicked
a bottle across the sand.

Suddenly he noticed a message inside the bottle. It was an S.O.S!

We are castaways on DEAD MAN'S ISLAND. Come quick and save us! Signed: Mum and Dad

Jumping Jellyfish!

Portside thought that the
note seemed *unusually* scruffy.
But no one else stopped to
look that closely.

Patch and Peg were already
racing off to the rescue.
"Avast, my hearties," cried Patch.
"Raise the anchor! And hoist the
main sail!"

When they got to Dead Man's Island, Patch couldn't see any sign of Mum and Dad's ship. The island *looked* deserted.

Patch didn't wait for a second.
He raced to the rescue,
followed by Granny Peg.
They ran straight into . . .

. . . their old enemies:
Bones and Jones.

In less time than it took for
Peg's knitting to slip off its
needles, Patch and his crew were
tied up and locked in a cabin . . .

. . . all except Pierre.
Bones and Jones had a job for
him! They told the parrot to
take a ransom note to Patch's
mum and dad. It said:

We've got your kid and his granny.
Bring us all your gold and guineas...
OR ELSE!

"Now, off you go," growled Bones.
"And don't be slow!" added Jones.
Then the scurvy pair laughed,
"Or your friends are fish food!"

Outside the cabin, Bones and
Jones were keeping watch . . .

. . . and arguing,
as usual.

"This was my best idea – *ever!*"
boasted Bones.
"This was *my* best idea – ever!"
insisted Jones.

Inside the cabin Patch was worried. What would Mum and Dad say when they found out he'd gone to sea, instead of going to school?

He had to escape – but how?
Patch had no ideas, nor did Peg.
Luckily, Portside had a plan.

As well as being the cleverest sea dog ever to sail the seven seas, Portside was also the best digging dog on dry land!

In a flash he had dug his
way out of the cabin and
back onto the island.

Then the *ingenious* dog
dug two more holes.

When he had finished, Portside began to bark.
He barked and barked until Bones and Jones came running from different directions.

They were running so fast they
bumped straight into each other
and fell into two . . .

. . . big holes.

The Little Pearl soon set sail.
Patch had to be home before
Mum and Dad got back.

On their way, everyone wondered
where poor Pierre was right now.

But when they got home,
they were glad to find a rather
bedraggled parrot waiting
for them.

Luckily, the clever Pierre had managed to lose the ransom note somewhere at sea.

"Towering Turbot!" whistled Patch. What a capable crew he had.

Later, when Mum and Dad came home, they told Patch and Peg how they'd rescued two pirates from Dead Man's Island.

"Called Bones and Jones," said
Mum. "Ever heard of them?"
Peg shook her head. "Can't say
I have."
Patch wisely
said...nothing.

★ Pirate Patch ★

ROSE IMPEY   NATHAN REED

All priced at £8.99

Orchard Colour Crunchies are available from all good bookshops,
or can be ordered direct from the publisher:
Orchard Books, PO BOX 29, Douglas IM99 1BQ
Credit card orders please telephone 01624 836000
or fax 01624 837033 or visit our internet site: www.orchardbooks.co.uk
or e-mail: bookshop@enterprise.net for details.

To order please quote title, author and ISBN
and your full name and address.
Cheques and postal orders should be made payable to 'Bookpost plc.'
Postage and packing is FREE within the UK
(overseas customers should add £2.00 per book).

Prices and availability are subject to change.

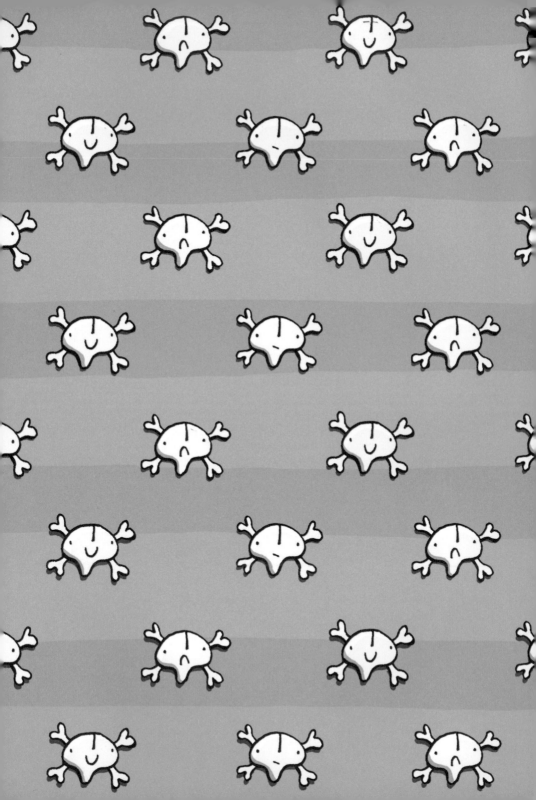